JUNGLE DRUM

DEANNA WUNDROW

CUT-PAPER ILLUSTRATIONS BY
SUSAN SWAN

The Millbrook Press
Brookfield, Connecticut

For my brother, Paul

—Deanna

For Terry, with love

—Susan

Published by The Millbrook Press, Inc.
2 Old New Milford Road
Brookfield, CT 06804

Text copyright © 1999 by Deanna Wundrow
Illustrations copyright © 1999 by Susan Swan
All rights reserved
Printed in the United States of America
5 4 3 2 1

Original art photographed by Terry Rasberry

Library of Congress Cataloging-in-Publication Data
Wundrow, Deanna.
Jungle drum / Deanna Wundrow : illustrated by Susan Swan.
p. cm.
Summary: The rain forest is filled with the sounds of the echoing jungle
drum, dripping water, and the many animals talking.
ISBN 0-7613-1270-6 (lib. bdg.)
[1. Rain forests—Fiction. 2. Rain forest animals—Fiction. 3. Sound—Fiction.]
I. Swan, Susan Elizabeth, ill. II. Title.
PZ7.W96377Ju 1999
[Fic]—dc21   98-12886 CIP AC

The jungle drum talks. It says,
"Ba-da doom. Ba-da doom doom, Ba-da doom.
Ba-da doom doom..."

All of the jungle animals are quiet.
They are listening to the jungle drum.
"Ba-da doom. Ba-da doom doom, Ba-da doom.
Ba-da doom doom...Ba-da Doom!"

The jungle drum is silent. The jungle is quiet.
Nothing moves.
All of the animals are listening.
They hear the sound of trees growing.

Then, a water drop
drops into a pool of
water.

It says, "Blip!"

And another
one answers,
"Blop!"

A mosquito, resting on a twig, begins to fly.
She says, "Hmmmmmmmm…?"

A tree frog, climbing up a tree,
puffs out his throat and croaks,
"Creeeeeeee, creeeeeeee!"

And then a million insects all at once begin to sing
chirp buzz whine scream. "Sst Sst Chei! Sst Sst Chei!"
"Breeeeeem Breeeeeem…" "S-churrrrrrrr!"
"Eow-eow-eow-eow…" "Pru-pru-pru!"

Now the jungle is very noisy. Everyone is talking!

Up in the canopy, parrots are screeching.
"Kahrooo! Kahrooo chooo!"
And the trees are full of monkeys chattering.
"Eee-eee? Oh-oh Ooh!"

On the ground, wild boars make a snorting sound.
"Snurrrrr…Snuff! Snurrrrr…"

And deep in the jungle a jaguar growls,
"Grrr-r-r-r-rhhh!"

Even the jungle drum begins talking again. It says, "Ba-da doom. Ba-da doom doom, Ba-da doom. Ba-da doom doom..."

The jaguar stops growling.
He is listening to the drum.

All of the animals stop to listen.
The wild boar stops snorting.
The monkeys stop chattering.
The parrots stop screeching.
The insects stop singing, chirping, buzzing,
whining, screaming.
The tree frog stops croaking.
And the mosquito. . . stops . . . humming.

All of the animals are quiet. They are all
listening. "Ba-da doom. Ba-da doom doom,
Ba-da doom. Ba-da doom doom…"

The jungle drum is silent. The jungle is quiet.

Then two water drops drop...
"Blip!"
"Blop!"

And a mosquito says,
"Hmmmmmmmmm...?"

Eee-eee . . .

Hmmmmmmmm . . .

MOSQUITO

MONKEYS

WILD BOAR

PARROTS

Kahrooo Chooo

Snurrrr snuff . . .

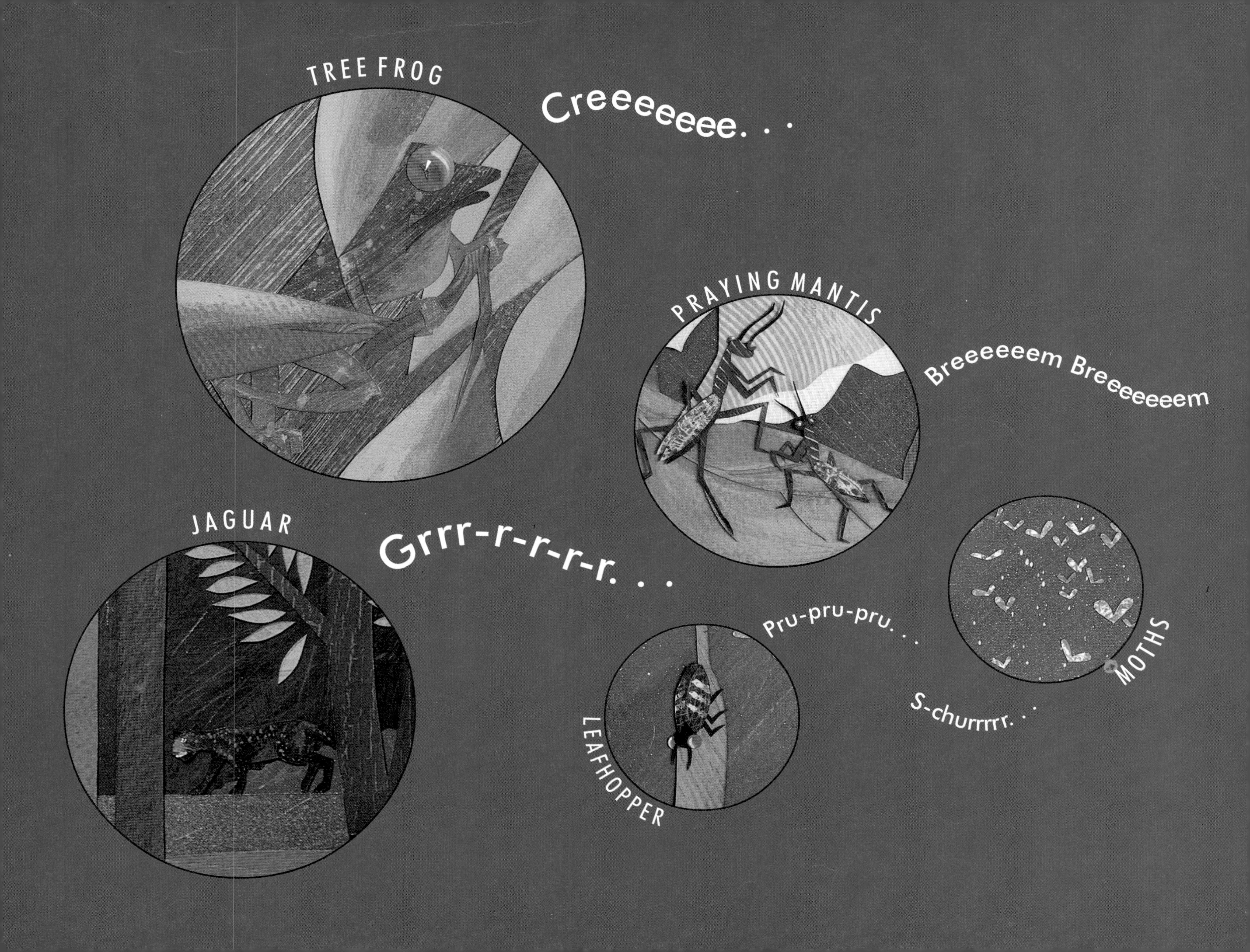

TREE FROG

Creeeeee. . .

PRAYING MANTIS

Breeeeeem Breeeeeem

JAGUAR

Grrr-r-r-r. . .

Pru-pru-pru. . .

MOTHS

S-churrrrr. . .

LEAFHOPPER

DEANNA WUNDROW grew up in San Diego, where she now lives with her husband, Guillermo. In 1992, while living in Costa Rica, she took a trip into the tropical rainforest. With a plastic tarp to keep off the rain, she backpacked through remote areas, and marveled at the abundance of life. The dense vegetation made it difficult to see the animals, but the sounds they made were incredible – as beautiful and mysterious as the rainforest itself.

SUSAN SWAN usually creates three-dimensional paper sculptures, but for this book she used a flat cut-paper style. First she selected her papers and hand-painted them, to get the rich colors and textures she wanted for the jungle and animals. Then she went to work creating each piece of art, layering the cut-paper to give a feeling of depth and to draw the reader in. Finally, Susan's husband, Terry, photographed the finished artwork, with lighting that accented the shadows of the paper. Susan and her husband are, professionally, Swan & Rasberry Studios, and they live in Texas.